SNOWMAN SNOWDOWN

Written by Joy Brewster

SCHOLASTIC INC.

New York Toronto London Auckland Sydney
Mexico City New Delhi Hong Kong Buenos Aires

ISBN 0-439-55712-7

Designed by Louise Bova

12 11 10 9 8 7 6 5 4 3 2 1   4 5 6 7 8 9/0

Special thanks to Duendes del Sur
for cover and interior illustrations.

Printed in the U.S.A.
First printing, February 2004

Chapter 1

The Mystery Machine drove up a long road. The gang saw green valleys below, and tall mountains above.

A huge ski resort was built on the mountain. Ski trails led down the mountain to a large, stone lodge.

Fred turned the van through the big stone gates. "Ah, the Vista Ski Lodge," he sighed. "Home of the

Swift Snowboarding Open. All my boarding heroes will be there."

"And so will all my favorite food," said Shaggy. "Hot chocolate, hot-cakes, hotdogs. "

Fred parked the van outside the lodge. Then the gang turned on the van's TV.

A reporter came on the screen. "This is Nancy Chang with Channel 10 News," she said. A shiny hel-

icopter landed behind her. "We're waiting to talk to the founder of the Swift Snowboarding Open, computer billionaire Sam Swift."

A man with gray hair stepped off the helicopter. Nancy Chang rushed over to him. "Mr. Swift, we've heard that Olympic champion Chris Klug was hurt in a mysterious way," she started. "How will this loss affect the games?"

"Nancy," Mr. Swift said with a smile. "I'm sure with a million-dollar prize, the other snowboarders will be hungry for victory."

"I think we should have a little talk with Chris Klug," Daphne said.

The gang found the Olympic champ in the ski lodge. He was sitting by a big stone fireplace. His arm was tied up in a sling. GET WELL SOON baskets filled with food surrounded him.

"I'm bummed I won't be shredding the powder here," Chris told the gang. "No thanks to that supersized snow creature."

"You were attacked by a snow creature?" Velma asked.

"Creepy, huh?" Chris said. He made a face.

Fred scratched his head. "Hmmm," he began. "The best way to get a handle on the mystery is from the *inside*. I'll pretend to be one of the pro boarders!"

"But Freddie," Daphne said. "What about the monster?"

Just then, the famous snow-boarder Avalanche Anderson walked up. He had just come off the slopes. He was covered with melting snow. Avalanche was older than the other snowboarders, but he was still one of the best. "Monster?" he asked. "Freaky."

"Avalanche Anderson!" Fred cried. "You practically *invented* the sport. I've been watching your movies since I was a kid!"

Now Daphne was impressed. "You're a movie star?" she asked.

"No, no," Avalanche shook his head. "I just did some action movies with snowboarding chases."

All of a sudden, a huge BURP came from one of the food baskets.

Scooby popped out of the basket. His belly was swollen from all the food. "Rorry," he said.

"Scooby just might need that extra fuel," laughed Fred. "We're going to search every trail for that Snow Creature!"

Chapter 2

That night, the gang hiked along the main trail up the mountain. They were wearing their warmest snow gear. The only light came from the moon and their flashlights.

"Shh," Fred whispered. "Someone's coming."

The gang hid quietly behind a few trees. A mysterious figure was creeping through the woods. It had an odd-shaped head and large hands. When it got closer, they saw two glowing red eyes.

"Row Reature!" gasped Scooby.

"Let's follow him!" Fred whispered.

The gang quietly followed the figure through the woods. Suddenly, they heard a strange rumble.

"Scooby, is that your stomach?" Velma asked.

"Ruhh-ruh," Scooby replied.

"Well, what do you think it is?" Daphne whispered.

Shaggy bumped into something. He looked up to see the Snow Creature standing right in front of him!

The Snow Creature let out a loud roar. The gang froze. Then everyone ran in different directions.

The Snow Creature chased after

Fred through the woods. Fred ran
as fast as he could. But the Snow
Creature kept getting closer and
closer. Suddenly, Fred tripped and
tumbled down the hill. He landed
headfirst in a pile of snow.

"Ughhh," he moaned.

A large, dark figure appeared. Was it the Snow Creature again? Fred struggled to get up, but he felt an awful pain. "Owww!" he cried. "My leg!"

Fred found his flashlight and shined it on the stranger's face.

"Hey!" the man yelled. "Get that outta my face!"

Fred was surprised to see an old man, not a monster. The man had a shaggy beard and wore overalls.

The gang ran over. "What's going on?" Daphne said.

"Your friend here just broke his leg," the old man grumbled.

"Who are you?" Velma asked.

"Theodore," the old man

answered with a grunt. "I'm the
trail manager."

Velma looked at the old man
closely. "Didn't you just see the
Snow Creature?"

"Aw, quit yer crazy talk,"
Theodore said. "Help me get your
friend into my snow tractor."

Chapter 3

Back at the lodge, the gang met in Fred's room. Fred's leg was in a cast.

"I think we might need to take a closer look at our friend Theodore," Daphne said.

Velma wiped her runny nose. "Yeah," she said. "He showed up just after we saw the Snow Creature. Why?"

"Good point!" Fred said. "Let's

check him out!" He started to get up, but his crutches fell to the floor.

"You're not going anywhere!" Daphne told him. "You're going to rest, just like the doctor said. We'll go investigate."

Everyone but Fred hiked the trail to Theodore's cabin. When they arrived, Velma knocked loudly. "Anyone home?" she called.

No one answered, so Velma opened the door slowly. The small cabin was dark and gloomy. It was almost empty, with only a few old things scattered around.

"Ah-ah-ah-CHOOOO!" Velma sneezed. Then she pointed at a clue. "Look!" A few old newspapers were tacked to the wall.

"Ski tragedy . . ." read Daphne. "Champion ski jumper Theodore Shushman's career was cut short. He ran into a young man on a new invention called a 'snowboard' . . ."

"Jinkies," Velma said. "A ski jumping champion whose career was cut short by a snowboarder. He must not like all these young snowboarders around."

All of a sudden, there was a loud rumble. The rumble turned to a roar. The gang rushed to the door and saw the Snow Creature stomping through the woods.

"Zoinks!" yelled Shaggy. "I tell ya, that is definitely NOT a jolly snowman!"

A cry came from the woods: "Ahhhh! Help! Monster!"

The gang raced through the woods. They found Avalanche Anderson sprawled in a pile of snow.

Back at the lodge, the doctor checked Avalanche's ankle.

"I'm telling you, doc," the champ explained. "The monster was made of snow and ice. It . . . Ow!!"

"That ankle's pretty hurt," the

doctor said. "We should have it
X-rayed."

"What's the point," Avalanche
said sadly. "I'm out of the running
for the championship."

Nearby, the gang had tracked
down Sam Swift.

"Will you kids leave me alone?"

the billionaire yelled. "I've got enough problems with my star boarders hurt!"

"Please listen," Daphne pleaded. "Fred's plan is brilliant!"

The creature is trying to injure pro boarders," Fred explained. "If we can put someone into the competition to *pretend* to be a top boarder, we can set a trap."

"This Snow Creature stuff is a lot of fluff," Mr. Swift declared. "But if it will get you kids off my back, fine!" He walked off in a huff.

"I don't get it, Fred," Shaggy said. "With your busted ankle, who's going to be the bait?"

"Reah, rho?" Scooby asked.

Fred looked at Shaggy and smiled.

Chapter 4

"No. Nope. No way. Not gonna happen," Shaggy said. He shook his head wildly.

Daphne and Shaggy were on top of the mountain looking down at the slope. Daphne wore skis. Shaggy stood on a snowboard. He was dressed like a pro boarder.

"Come on, Shaggy," Daphne begged. "It's not like you really have to snowboard. All you have to do is fake it and wait for that creature to come after you!"

"Oh yeah," Shaggy said. "That's *much* better."

"Hmm," Daphne said. "I have an idea. Open wide and say 'ah!'"

Shaggy opened his mouth. Daphne poured in a bag of Scooby Snacks. Shaggy gobbled them up as fast as he could.

"Oh-chay!" he said with a mouthful.

A group of snowboarders piled off the chairlift.

"Here they come," Daphne said. "Catch you later!"

Daphne pulled down her goggles and skied away.

One of the snowboarders, Kay

Muller, swooped in on her board. She sprayed snow on Shaggy.

"So, you are the amazing boarder we've been hearing about?" she said.

Shaggy gulped his last snack. "Ulp, yup, that's me," he said.

"Well," said Kay. "I will give you a little help." She pushed Shaggy lightly on the back.

Shaggy flew down the slope. "Zoooooinks!" he screamed.

Shaggy sped down the slope waving his arms. He went over a little hill of snow and flew into the air. He landed with a THUMP! Before he could catch his breath, he hit another mound of snow. This one was even bigger and sent him into a flip. He landed on his feet!

Just as he was starting to have fun, Shaggy heard an awesome ROAR! The Snow Creature was right behind him. The frozen monster was stirring up a cloud of snow as he chased Shaggy.

"Zoinks!" Shaggy shouted.

Shaggy was boarding as fast as he could. But the Snow Creature was getting closer and closer! Then Shaggy's board hit a patch of ice.

The board flew one way and Shaggy went flying the other way — right at the Snow Creature! "Help!" Shaggy cried.

Just then, Scooby raced up on a super-sized sled. He caught Shaggy in the air and zipped away.

"Like, nice catch!" Shaggy said.

Scooby turned the sled to the left, to the right, then headed right for . . . a frozen lake! They slid onto the ice and did a few spins. The Snow Creature stopped at the edge of the lake. He roared and shook his fists. But he was too heavy to walk on the ice.

"You totally saved us!" Shaggy yelled. "Like, thanks!"

Chapter 5

"Very interesting," Velma muttered. She was searching the Web for clues.

"What is it?" Daphne asked. She and Fred read the screen.

"Billionaire to Go Bust!" Fred read aloud.

Velma clicked on another page and read the headline: "Swift Empire Falls."

"Sounds like Sam Swift is losing his fortune," Daphne added.

"So, why is he acting like such a big spender?" Fred asked.

"Good question," said Velma. Then she let out a noisy "Ah-CHOO!"

Daphne handed Velma a warm blanket. "You're too sick to think," she said. "You need to rest."

Fred showed Velma a big stack of DVDs. "Hey, if you can't sleep, check out these old snowboarding movies," he said.

"Oh . . ." Velma moaned. "Lucky me . . ." She started snoring loudly.

Daphne walked to the window to close the curtains. "Freddie, look!" she cried. "There's a light at the top of the ski jump!"

Fred pulled out his night vision goggles. He could see flashing lights coming from the ski jump gate. Suddenly, a mysterious figure appeared. "Check it out!" Fred cried. "There's that weird figure we saw last night — right before the Snow Creature appeared."

Daphne took a look. "I wonder what he's doing there," she said.

"I'll go find out!" Fred declared. He jumped up from his seat. He forgot about his cast and landed with a THUD on the floor. "Ooooohhh," he moaned.

"You're not going anywhere, mister," Daphne demanded.

"Well, I guess I can watch you

from here," Fred replied. "I'll call your cell phone if I see anything. But be careful!"

Before long, Daphne was zipping up the slopes in a snowmobile. She sent snow spraying behind her.

"Yeeee-haaaaa!" she hollered.

RRRRING. RRRRING. Daphne picked up her cell phone. "Hello?"

"You call that careful?" Fred yelled. He was watching her through his night-vision goggles.

Daphne pulled up to the ski jump gate. "Hang on, Freddie," she said. She parked her snowmobile and walked into the old shack by the gate. "Hey, what's this?" From the outside, the shed looked run-down. But inside, there were high-tech computers, electronic machines, and speakers.

Fred watched through his goggles. A big shape appeared near the door. The Snow Creature!

"Daphne!" Fred yelled into the phone. "Get out of there!"

But Daphne only heard static. "Freddie?" she called. "What did you say? I didn't catch that!"

Daphne turned to step outside. THUD! She walked right into a wall of . . . ice? It was the Snow Creature!

"Jeepers!" she whispered. "I think I just got the message!"

ROAR! The Snow Creature shook its icy fists at Daphne, but

she slammed the door in its face.
The monster shattered the door
with a mighty blow.

Daphne scrambled to the back of
the shed. She looked through her
backpack and pulled out a travel
hair dryer. She pointed it at the
Snow Creature. "Eat the heat,
slush-face!"

The Snow Creature stomped closer and closer. It wasn't melting!

Daphne looked around for another way to escape. She saw a hole in the roof covered with ice and snow. She pointed her dryer up at the hole. In seconds, the ice and snow landed with a THUMP — right on the Snow Creature!

Daphne ran outside and jumped on her snowmobile.

Fred watched her zoom away. He tried the cell phone again. This time, Daphne answered. "Hello?" she said.

"Cool getaway, Daph," Fred said.

"You mean HOT getaway, Freddie!" Daphne laughed.

Chapter 6

"Hey, pass the hot sauce, Scoob," Shaggy said.

He and Scooby had snuck into the ski lodge kitchen. They found some leftover soup. Shaggy was adding a few more ingredients: hot sauce, hot chilies, and hot peppers.

Velma stumbled through the door. She was still red and puffy from her cold. "I thought I'd find you two here," she said.

At that moment, voices came from outside the door.

"Hey, like I don't think we're supposed to be here this late!" Shaggy whispered.

Velma, Shaggy, and Scooby hid under the table, just before three people walked in: Sam Swift, Chris Klug, and Avalanche Anderson.

"Come on, guys!" Mr. Swift pleaded. "You just have to compete. The Swift Empire is counting on these games."

Avalanche shook his head. "Mr. Swift, even if we could climb on our boards, with Chris' broken arm and my twisted ankle . . ."

"It would be good-bye to our careers!" Chris said. "Sorry, rich dude. No can do."

The three men walked through the back doors out the kitchen.

"Whew!" Velma sighed. "That was close! Let's go find Fred and Daphne."

Back in their room, the gang paced back and forth. They couldn't figure out the mystery.

"Mr. Swift seemed pretty desperate," Velma said.

"He doesn't seem to care that Chris and Avalanche are hurt," Daphne said. "But who's behind the Snow Creature?"

"Well, the snowboarders have motives," Shaggy said. "Like, a one million dollar motive to be exact!"

"But they're the ones who are getting attacked by the Snow Creature!" Fred said.

"We can't forget about creepy old Theodore," Shaggy said.

"Right!" Velma said. "Or that mystery sneak we saw up on the mountain. He keeps showing up right before the Snow Creature."

"We just need something to trap the Snow Creature," Fred said.

"Or some*one*!" Daphne said.

Velma, Daphne, and Fred looked at Shaggy and Scooby.

"Oh, no," Shaggy said. "There's NOTHING that would make Scooby and me agree to a face-to-face with that icy beast."

Chapter 7

"I tell you, pal," Shaggy said to Scooby. "One of these days I'm going to say NO to Scooby Snacks."

Shaggy and Scooby were walking up a snowy mountain path in search of the Snow Creature.

"Re roo!" Scooby agreed.

Shaggy started to shout into the woods: "Yoo-hoo! Snow Creature! Come out, come out, whatever you are!"

"Rhee-hee-hee," Scooby giggled.

Shaggy felt a tap on his shoulder. "Not now, Scoob," Shaggy said. "I'm on a roll. Hey, Snow Cone Head!"

An awful sound came from right behind them. "ROAR!"

Shaggy slowly turned around. "Run!" he screamed, jumping into Scooby's arms.

Scooby and Shaggy raced away as fast as they could. "HEEELLLLLPP!" they screamed.

At the bottom of the slopes, Fred was showing Velma and Daphne his trap. "Then Velma pulls the rope, and this barrel will topple over onto Mr. Frosty. Then Daphne blasts him with the snow-making machine!"

"Here they come!" Daphne cried.

Shaggy and Scooby came sliding down the mountain. The Snow Creature was right behind them.

"Like, gangway!" yelled Shaggy.

Velma couldn't hold in her sneeze any more: "AHHH-CHOOOOOO!" She yanked the rope too early. The barrel landed with a THUMP on top of Scooby and Shaggy.

They scrambled out from under it just in time to roll it at the Snow Creature. The Snow Creature went flying into the air. It came crashing to the ground.

Velma opened a clear, plastic door in the Snow Creature's back and found the OFF switch. The see-through creature screeched to a stop.

"So Mr. Frosty Freeze was a fake after all!" Shaggy said.

"That's why I couldn't melt him with my hair dryer!" Daphne cried.

Velma took a closer look at the plastic monster on the ground. "This is really a remote-controlled device, like in the movies," she said.

"He's made entirely out of some kind of clear plastic," Fred said. "It looks just like ice!"

"But who is controlling him?" Shaggy asked.

"Look!" Daphne cried. She pointed up toward the ski jump gate. "Up there!"

A mysterious figure was starting down the ski jump.

"It's that mystery sneak!" Shaggy yelled. "He's getting away!"

Scooby had an idea. He sprinkled pepper in front of Velma's face.

Sure enough, Velma crinkled her nose and let out a huge sneeze: "AHHH-AHHH-AHHH-AHHH-CHOOOOOO!" It was her biggest sneeze yet. The sound echoed: "CHOOO!" "CHOOO!" "CHOOO!"

The sound bounced around, starting a small avalanche. The

snow poured down the mountain after the mystery figure. He fell and landed in a pile of snow. His face was covered by a ski mask. An electric helmet lay beside him.

"Now," Fred started. "Let's find out who this mystery person is." Fred pulled off the mask.

"Avalanche Anderson?!" everybody cried.

Chapter 8

A crowd gathered around to see what was happening. Chris Klug and Sam Swift stepped forward.

"We knew the creature had to be a machine," Velma explained. "There were tire marks all over the mountain."

"But how did he make the Snow Creature so real?" Shaggy asked.

"With these," Fred started. He switched the creature back on.

Then he put on the helmet and gloves Avalanche had been wearing. "Avalanche controlled the monster with this Virtual Reality helmet and these gloves. That's why it moved and acted like a real, living creature." As Fred moved his hand up and down, the creature's hand moved the same way.

"How did you know it was Avalanche?" Mr. Swift asked.

"When I was sick, I watched some old snowboarding movies," Velma said. "Avalanche was in almost every one. I knew he must know a lot of people in Hollywood."

"And people who know all about special effects," Daphne said.

"Exactly," Velma nodded.

Chris Klug looked confused. "But Avalanche," he said. "Why?"

"Because of hotshot kids like you!" Avalanche replied. "I used to be the best in the world! I wanted that back! The only thing standing in my way was you!"

"But we saw him wounded by the creature!" Shaggy said.

"No, we saw him lying in the snow," Velma said. "He told us he

was attacked. Avalanche was about to pretend to make a quick recovery, just in time for the games."

"And with the rest of us out, he would've won the money AND the fame!" Chris Klug added.

"If it weren't for those meddling kids, I'd be famous again!" Avalanche cried, shaking his fists.

Fred dialed his cell phone. "Oh, you'll be famous all right," he said. "With the police."

That afternoon, the games began. Chris Klug and the gang stood at the top of the mountain. They were watching snowboarders zip down the slopes.

"You know," Chris said to Shaggy. "You're still entered in the contest.

Why don't you take a run? I brought a board up for you." He handed Shaggy a snowboard.

"Uhh-uh," Shaggy said, shaking his head. "No way! I've had enough scary runs this season. Nothing, and I mean NOTHING, could get me down the slope."

Suddenly, they heard a deep growl. They turned and saw the Snow Creature's head appear from behind a mound of snow.

"Well, maybe ONE thing!" Shaggy cried. He grabbed the snowboard and tore off down the slope. "Like, later!"

Scooby popped his head up next to the Snow Creature's. He was wearing the Virtual Reality helmet

and gloves. As he giggled, it looked
like the Snow Creature giggled too.
　Together, Scooby and the Snow
Creature did a little dance.
"Scooby-dooby-doooo!"